BOOKS BY NORMAN DUBIE

Groom Falconer

W · W · NORTON & COMPANY · NEW YORK · LONDON

Groom Falconer

POEMS BY Norman Dubie

Acknowledgment is due the following publications, in which these poems first appeared:

The American Poetry Review: "Ars Poetica"; "Baptismal"; "Poem"; "Groom Falconer"; "Jeremiad"; "Trakl"; "The Death of the Race Car Driver"; "Coyote Creek"; "Victory"; "Accident"; "The Peace of Lodi"; "Chagall"; "The Wine Bowl"; "Near the Bridge of Saint-Cloud"; "The Clergyman's Daughter"; "Amen"; "The Garden Asylum of Saint-Paul-de-Mausole"; "The Fish"; "Of Politics, & Art"; "The Desert Deportation of 1915."
Santa Monica Review: "Easter Night, Paris."
Western Humanities Review: "Union Ushers at the Norcross Farm."
Quarterly West: " 'They are the Queens of the Bird's Body' "; "An American Scene"; "First Wednesday at Heater Lawns."
Field: "Buffalo Clouds over the Maestro Hoon"; "The Apocrypha of Jacques Derrida."
The Mississippi Review: "Shrine"; "Encanto's Ferry."
Gettysburg Review: "Northwind Escarpment"; "Shipwreck."
Hayden's Ferry Review: "Fever"; "New Age at Airport Mesa"; "Safe Conduct"; "The Saints of Negativity."
Argos, Wales: "At the Opening to the Underground Cemetery at Colchis."

"Near the Bridge of Saint-Cloud" is dedicated to David Sklar. "Ars Poetica" is for Tito and Lupita. "The Fish" is for Michael Berman.

My thanks to the Ingram Merrill Foundation for their generosity without which this book would not have been completed.

Published simultaneously in Canada by Penguin Books Canada Ltd., 2801 John Street, Markham, Ontario L3R 1B4.
Printed in the United States of America.

The text of this book is composed in Bulmer, with display type set in Bauer Bodoni. Composition by The Maple-Vail Book Manufacturing Group. Manufacturing by The Haddon Craftsmen Inc.

First Edition
Library of Congress Cataloging-in-Publication Data
Dubie, Norman, 1945–
    Groom falconer : poems / Norman Dubie.—1st ed.
      p.   cm.
    I. Title.
    PS3554.U255G76   1989
    811'.54—dc19   88–19570

ISBN 0-393-02662-0

W. W. Norton & Company, Inc., 500 Fifth Avenue, New York, N. Y. 10110
W. W. Norton & Company ltd., 37 Great Russell Street, London WC1B 3NU

1 2 3 4 5 6 7 8 9 0

For Hannah

Contents

O N E

T W O

T H R E E

ONE

Wandering, estranged and lonely, he saw a wild
pig covered with mud, and a wagon full of
demons. First he stretched his bow but then put
it aside. It is not an obstacle, but a matter of
betrothal to the times. . . .

—*I Ching*

Ars Poetica

It is almost polio season. The girls

From the cigarette factories in Massachusetts
Are still visiting the northern beaches.
At midnight, the milky rubbers
In the breakers are like a familiar invasion

Of sea life.
Sitting on the rocks we watch a runner:
Weight shifted, some *tick, tick,*
Almost of intelligence—
The bone catching of balance . . .

From behind, a red-haired girl appears—
Missing a thumb on her left hand,
Breathless, she asks for a light:
A crumpled pack of Lucky Strikes
At the top of a nylon stocking;
The other leg bare, her abdomen
And breasts plastered with white sand.
Drunk, she says, "He just swam out
Past the jetty—that was twenty minutes
Ago. You think I give a damn."

We lit the cigarette for her. Her hands
Shaking.

No moon, it took an hour
To find all her clothing,
Dropped as they ran
Down the rock shelf through dunes . . .

3

He hadn't drowned. He swam around the jetty,
Crawled to the grasses and over the granite shelf.
Gathering his clothes, he left
Her there as a joke.

Her hair was colored
That second chaste coat of red on the pomegranate.
We were eating sandwiches on the rocks.
She frightened my mother and me. My little
Sister just thought she was funny.
In thirty years I have dreamt of her twice, once
With fear and once without. I've written
This for her, and because

Twice is too often
Considering how beautiful she was.

Baptismal

The lightning inside the black cloud put slabs
Of amethyst in the sky. We took the wine
And went inside the old garden house for shelter.
Anne had gone to a cremation that Friday. She said
That in the heat
All the rope in the corpse shortens and dries,
The body slowly rises to a sitting position,
And in the updraft of the furnace
The hair stands on end. Then, the hair burns, she said.

Bill smiled, saying, "That's a lie, Anne." When I was nine,
Anne responded, we stood over
The old Water Street cemetery. The grass
Wasn't cut and it had been a wet spring
Followed by a long dry summer.
We threw in three matches. Beth, in a simple print dress,
With the wind rising, wet herself and
Took down her panties tossing them into the fire.
The rows of soapstone crosses
Wilted in the flames. Above it all stood
Some smoke blackened statuary:
A bronze eagle wrestling with a marble snake
And to the north, large female angels
With breasts and extended wings, their attention
Was on the snake
And in the shimmering heat they began
To walk over the fire like a lake.

Poem

A mule kicked out in the trees. An early
Snow was falling,
The girl walked across the field
With a hairless doll, she dragged
It by the green corduroy of its sleeve
And with her hands
Buried it beside the firepond.

The doll was large enough to make a mound
Which she patted down a dozen times.
Then she walked back alone.
The weak winter sun
Sat on the horizon like a lacquered mustard seed.

She never noticed me
Beside the road drinking tea from a thermos.
The noisy engine cooling.
Did you ever want to give someone

All your money? We drove past midnight, ate,
And drove some more—unable to sleep in Missouri.

Trakl

—for Paul & Doug

In reality the barn wasn't clean, ninety men
Charged to you:
The burns, missing teeth, and dark jawbone
Of gnawed corn, gangrene from ear to elbow—
Even the dying
Returned to consciousness by the ammonia of cows.

You ran out looking beyond your hands
To the ground, above you a wind
In the leaves: looking up you found
Hanged partisans convulsing in all the trees.

Down the road in the garrison hospital,
In a cell for the insane, you were given
Green tea and cocaine . . .
With the blue snow of four o'clock
Came peace and that evening of memory
With Grete, her touch—in yellow spatterdock
She tied a black ribbon
Around the cock of a sleeping horse.
It was her *vivacious littles* as an admirer
Once put it. *Sister, trough. . . .*

How men talk. I read you first
In an overly heated room
Sitting in an open window. I left
For a walk in woods. Coming out
Into a familiar sinkhole, meadow
Now snow, deer ran over the crust—
Hundreds of them. I thought of my two uncles,

Their war, the youngest dead at Luzon,
The other, in shock,

7

At his barracks in California: Christmas evening
He looked up from the parade grounds and saw
An old Japanese prisoner
With arms raised, from the hands came
A pigeon. The bird climbed, climbed
Slowly and then dissolved

Like smoke from some lonely howitzer
Blossoming out over the bubbling bone pits of lye, over
The large sunken eyes of horticulture.

Jeremiad

After a night of opium and alcohol, Edgar Poe
Walks out of a laundry into the harsh sunlight
Of an affluent Baltimore. From behind, as I see him,
He is not
Of experience, and he is without sin—
He waddles
In the archetype of Charlie Chaplin
And crosses the street to the park
Where yesterday evening yellow swathes of poison
Were dropped on the wind
To kill an unprecedented population
Of ground snails.

Now, Poe is reaching the great lawn of the park
Where swans have been feasting
On the tainted snails. The swans are sick.
Poe, drugged as he is,
Shatters with this vision of vomiting swans. He turns,

And running at him
In a line fifty yards long
Is a pack of stray dogs from everywhere
In Baltimore. They will eat the swans.

Edgar Allan Poe, who stood between them,
Made a judgment—

The hounds of hell were coming for him;
He climbed the statue of a stylish general
On a rearing horse.
He clung to the marble thigh of the stallion.
He watched, in horror, the field below him.
The torn swans were long syllables

Over the ground.
By the time he was able to climb down,
A crowd had formed. He told them, wide-eyed,

He told them what he saw—truth and beauty
Fornicating on the public lawn. Everyone frowned

As they sometimes will in Baltimore.

Groom Falconer

—circa 1903

Out walking along the river
I still saw the fever with her children
At supper in the coal light. Snow falling,
I climbed up through the wood
To the asylum to visit with Sister
In the locked ward. But hesitated
And went to the cottage to see the insomniac

Rich child who sits naked at the window:

Last night, in kerosene light, her back
Had a quality of milkglass. She curls
In the chair.
Her knees under her chin, the room black—

The light at the window is all
Moon and snow. She is at it again:

With the nail of the little finger
She has flayed
The thumb of the same hand;
All but the little finger arthritic
With the procedure: the raw thumb

White like a boiled egg
In an upturned palm; the dead skin,
Bits of shell, not polished by hen straw.

Beyond the window there is a sudden
Convulsion of wind in the blue spruce,
Boughs dumping snow. *I imagine*
The brass makeweights that lift the other pan,
Or this past summer, dust and pollen

11

Rising around oxslaughter. A shudder
Passes through the child, taking
Her attention;

She cuts herself for the first time, a trickle
Of blood at the knuckle of the thumb
Like the single red thread
Through the lace hood and jesses
Of the Medici falcons.
Her concentration broken, the hand
Loosens: *one wing, one stone.*

The sun is seeping over the snow.

She greets me with an acknowledgment
One reserves for a ghost.

The Death of the Race Car Driver

I have not slept for a week.

It is matchless—this feeling
I have for the dream:

Baled hay burning in the air
With the splintering planks of the barricade.
As I roll
I feel all over me, the silk drapery
Of boney French schoolgirls.

In the last month of the war,
Visiting a friend, I watched
A young nurse
Stare mindlessly past me
While soaping the testicles
Of an unconscious amputee . . .

At a hundred and eighty miles per hour
There's a little vibration in the chassis, a clarity
Like the musical waterglass
Gently tapped, but, here, silent and empty—
Speed and sleep have overlapped. My body,

Sack for eternity.

Fever

—for my wife

In your sleep you talked.

There are cows standing in white mud.
A bale of hay has fallen out of the sky for them.
The cows are rejoicing,
Standing on their hind legs.
Their rough teats caked
With the white mud.
Their great skulls above the ground fog.

While you talked I bathed you with a sponge
From a basin of ice and alcohol.
I told you that in my childhood,
During the mud season, old boards ran from the house
To the barns and then out into pastureland . . .

The farmer's wife is walking
On the old boards out to the dancing cows.
She's pissed and wants their milk.
Another bale of hay
Is falling from the sky. It's killed the farmer's wife.
Good enough for her.
The mud is sucking her down. Good-bye.

I said, "You know I love you."

Oh, my god, the farmer's wife is alive.
She's climbing out of the mud
Onto an old board. She looks like a tooth.
Oh, my god, she is a tooth.

I love you too.

14

Victory

The bed of the garden is black with nitrogen;
In fact, black with dried blood and meal.
Mary in a torn white gown
Walks out of the potatoes. She has sown

The winter wheat without a thought for the sparrows.
It's raining
On the yellow pond beyond the tannery.
It rains on the garden. Her work done
Mary spins her body clockwise,
Arms rising—there'll be winter wheat
In the bare ivy, in the neighbor's driveway . . .

Her mother calls without making a sound.
The girl turns for the house.

By ten o'clock she is scattering coal ashes
Over the sidewalk.
The chinaberry tree, heavy with ice,
Reflects the light from the window:
So the moon catches the sun, and the glassy shrub
A chandelier in the parlor. Mary reaches

Into the pockets of her father's brown coat.
He died last year of a hemorrhage.
She is all throat now, looking at stars:
If you stroked her, she would swallow the cosmos.

Union Ushers at the Norcross Farm

—1863

Our plane trees were made into ammunition crates
Leaving a stone house on bare earth.

In the cold noon, I withdrew
In two directions—
Into the dark house, but, also,
Out to the forsythia and beyond
To the red broken axles of the pinewood.

Looking down on the bare trees in early winter
I once saw the hours
Of a toothless ratchet clock
Become fire. It is all a dream of falling.

It's the cat dragging the flycatcher,
Broken breast and feathers,
Across a bulkhead below which
The potatoes sprout eyes in death.

The catbird buried under the forsythia, limned
And ragged, was once the measure
Of my tolerance for voices . . .

Now it is the war dead. Father
In satin, and the blue ushers
Smoking beside the barn. Their white gloves
On the bronze handrails of the coffin:
The swagger of the weight they share
Is obscene, I think, while waiting, breathless,
For my brain to clear. It is not the burial

That bothers me.
Last night I dreamt I was blinded by snow
Following a rope from the house to the barn.
Inside I smelled the animals.
I saw our servant girl stripped to the waist.
Her twin brother dead at Gettysburg.
She was on her back, in straw, under a cow.
Milk dragged through her red hair to her mouth:
Quick, Mistress, we must drink it now, or it'll sour!

Accident

He stood in a green stand of corn
And watched the light of a train
Shrink from the woods and crossing. It became
Absolute: at that last second, just a white dot
On the cab of the stalled truck in which
His daughter, foot off the clutch, fought gears.
The milk of field corn everywhere.
He fell back into the brittle stalks.
In the night an acetylene torch sputtered
Silencing the cicadas up in the cottonwoods.
The red caboose had mowed down corn
Stopping within ten feet of him.
Two men in overalls with a lantern
Stepped into the field.
They were from Mars. They opened their mouths,
Speaking in the one tongue of the blasted
Cattle cars, the cries
Of the dying animals strewn out behind them.

The Peace of Lodi

The South had to lose the war;
Lincoln had to be martyred if
healing was to occur.
*   —Ruth Ann Hastings*

One night, after a storm, the sort of storm
That is preceded by a sulphur calm—
Birds suddenly silent, people with lamps
Climbing down into cellars— one night,
After such a storm, driving the old Ford
Through the Iowa countryside, we stopped suddenly
Before the incandescent light of a tree
That had been shattered
By lightning— black and lavender
Amish surrounding a smouldering linden: they were
Just sitting in their buggies
Speaking to their horses in low voices
While an Elder, who had soaked his sleeves in water,
Lifted up out of the great charred circumference
Of the tree, a pail filled with boiling honey.
It was one of those infinite distances,
Yet finite as that thickness of glass
Between us and the assassin who stood behind Lincoln
In that wax museum across from the whorehouse
In Phoenix.

TWO

The Wine Bowl

There were dragons contending in the wilderness.

One tore open the throat of the other. Its death
Brought a late frost.
The next morning my mother came to us
With a frozen nest of yellow jackets.

It was the same spring, during the flowering,
That the Empress Dowager knelt in the dust
Of a hundred horsemen
And was made to drink poison.
They threw her body into the gorge.
The white geese were eaten for supper . . .

What I remember most from this season
Is the girl from the next village.
Her father made wine bowls.
She had a black mole on the side of her nose.
Her skin was translucent.
I sat in backwater and watched
Her and a friend
Bathe, one afternoon, out in the rushes:

The friend stepped out of the cold river,
The artisan's daughter laughed
And lay back on the water,
She floated past the green sandbar,
Where her friend was dressing,
Past the dark cranes eating crayfish,
Past the old wharves of my village,
And having joined the eternity of the river—
Evenings of drinking from the wine bowl—
She slowed,
Floating past me forever, her eyes closed.

Of Politics, & Art

Here, on the farthest point of the peninsula
The winter storm
Off the Atlantic shook the schoolhouse.
Mrs. Whitimore, dying
Of tuberculosis, said it would be after dark
Before the snowplow and bus would reach us.

She read to us from Melville.

How in an almost calamitous moment
Of sea hunting
Some men in an open boat suddenly found themselves
At the still and protected center
Of a great herd of whales
Where all the females floated on their sides
While their young nursed there. The cold frightened whalers
Just stared into what they allowed
Was the ecstatic lapidary pond of a nursing cow's
One visible eyeball.
And they were at peace with themselves.

Today I listened to a woman say
That Melville *might*
Be taught in the next decade. Another woman asked, "And why not?"
The first responded, "Because there are
No women in his one novel."

And Mrs. Whitimore was now reading from the Psalms.
Coughing into her handkerchief. Snow above the windows.
There was a blue light on her face, breasts and arms.
Sometimes a whole civilization can by dying
Peacefully in one young woman, in a small heated room
With thirty children
Rapt, confident and listening to the pure
God rendering voice of a storm.

The Apocrypha of Jacques Derrida

The ruptured underbelly of a black horse flew overhead.
Bonaparte, is what the matron said to me,
Always condescending; vulgar, slowly separating
The three syllables. And it was the last thing she said.
The engine block struck the tree. Our faces
Making brook ice of the windshield. The vaulting black horse
Now on its side in the dust. I was left
With the road, with the memory of cities burning.
Matron seemed to sleep. My nose bleeding.
I went over to inspect the huge sunflowers
That were beyond the stonewall. The sunflowers
Marched with me in Italy. They were cut down.
There was gasoline everywhere. The attendants
Will come for me. It's back to the island.
I'll study English out in the cool stucco of the shed.
I don't really believe I am the Corsican. But then
Neither did he.
The car was now burning with the tree. The black
Brook ice bursting. The horse got up and left.
A back hoof snared by intestine . . .

I was once all game leg in a fast sleigh
Passing a half-frozen cook who asked a frozen orderly,
"Is he the snow?"
If only that cook had been my general.
It was that straggling long line that cost us.
If they had moved in a dark swarm, huddled together,
Cloud shadow over the Russian countryside, then
There would have been little trouble, a few men
Out on the fringes dropping to the snow for rest,
But still how
Like a forest they would have been
Moving over the land

25

Like that gang who came for Macbeth.
I know what you're thinking, that the land pell-mell
Is itself mostly obstacle
And this makes a road. But we were cloud shadow

Moving over snow.

The Fish

A pale woman is cradling a large red fish
That she's stolen from the hospital kitchen.
She stands in the bright garden
In the cold wind. Black waterlilies
Are gently wrestling her to the gravel's edge.
In the struggle she kisses them
On their mouths. They say, sadly, "Alice, Alice!"
Grasping her red fish
At its banded anus, near the black spines
Of the tail, she knocks them
Unconscious with it. Even in their drowse
The waterlilies trouble Alice.
Her boss, Mr. Calvin, has had surgery—
Is dying now
In the freshly plastered solarium.
She'll be out of work by morning. Her sister
Thinks they are going to lose the house.
Alice was praying for a miracle. They drilled
Holes in his skull. And the red fish
Has fallen in with the waterlilies,
Into the small pond. It shivers, breaks
To the left, leaps into the air and, then,
Without a thought for Alice,
Swims toward the bottom to sleep in the mud.

Buffalo Clouds over the Maestro Hoon

—for our godson

It was a useless thing to do with the morning.

Couples with umbrellas strolled over the lawns
Beside the abyss.
The Maestro tossed a fresh bed of straw for his friend,
He sipped coffee with chicory,
And, then, attempted to walk over Niagra Falls
On a string while pushing a wheelbarrow
That contained a lion captured in the Congo.
Hoon had copper cleats
Sewn into his silk slippers. He wore the orange gown.
It was the full weight of the lion
That propelled this old man and wheelbarrow
Over the falls . . .

Of all things this is what
I've chosen to tell you about the world. This,
And the fact that bearded Hoon and his big cat
Faltered, again and again, up in the wind
But were not toppled.

It was a useless thing to do with the morning.
And a glory. The only beauty
In the story is that the lion roared. His voice
Twice lost to the deafening falls; of course,
It was reported that the lion yawned.
The courage of the beast, feigned or not,
Is a lesson in understanding us,
Who are right when we are wrong,
Who see boredom in a toothless lion,
In his *cri de coeur* over a stupefying volume
Of falling water

28

That sounds like the ovation
Given to Hoon as he stepped
Off his tightrope into the open arms
Of men and women with umbrellas
Still strange to one another while on their honeymoons.

Chagall

In the swollen rooms of the ghetto, the clicking
Of the aunts' knitting needles
Is the cool silver of your father's face, of the herring
He packed into tins all day.

Below the white cow, below the blood yoke,
Clouds grow with the laughter
Of young German soldiers.
They laugh while an officer
Fills the bladder of a fox
With water at the village spigot.

You shaved a little chalk into the color, thinned
It with oil from olives, then a vagabond whole-hearted woman
Appeared with the magic of boxed flowers.
She is as blissful as the new day . . .

At night, no bones left in her body, she sings
For her visitor
While floating on the pure blue jet of the bidet.

"They are the Queens of the Bird's Body"

—Eddie Miguel

The eagles have left the chalk of fish
Way up in the boughs of a salt cedar.
My mother lifts her skirt while standing
In the cold brook where the palomino is drinking.

We sleep in the burned-out Cadillac
When my father is drunk.
Grandmother is sad because Eisenhower
Died six months ago and nobody
Told her.
She makes a cake with apples in it.

The summer stars are not old.
The winter stars are,

And they are broken.
Mother says this is my opinion.

The skeletons of salmon up in the trees
Will be fatted with snow:
The strangest ones
Are the queens of the bird's body.

In last year's Christmas pageant, the snow
Was made of mica and sawdust,
Men emptied it from sacks while sitting

In the rafters of the Mission.
After the curtains closed, they swept it up
For the next performance. We went
To the candlelight service. The sawdust

Was falling again, but this time
With it, two coins, a mitten,
And, into the lap of the Virgin, a dry brown mouse.

Grandmother whispered, "This is a bad sign
In any religion."
And the Virgin
Still clutching her burning candle
Ran screaming from God's house.

Shrine

There is another
Hunt and another gentler
Hunter.

—John Logan

The sedan is a black grub with its strange mouth
Full of wood, the telegraph down, the truck
Rolls over in yellow brush and a burning bus
Is on its side in the bleached manure
Of an abandoned turkey farm.

The sky is so blue that it is cruel.

Seconds later Frieda comes down off the hill
And seeing a body— brakes,
She comes to a stop in the middle of the crossroads.
Nothing is moving.

She steps out onto the tar, the car door
Left open. She lifts the loose arm
Of the local grocer and lets it fall.
She scans the desert, thinking
Never in her life has she been alone.

It is quiet except for the burning bus
Which sounds like a wind
Without origin. The trees are still.
She walks
Down the white line, picking a straw hat
Up off the road. She chews on it. She knows
The sedan is eating pine. *Oh, jesus,*
She thought! And kept on walking . . .

They found her that night in the next town
Drinking coffee over pie. Somebody
Asked if she was all right. She said

She had followed her mind.

33

Encanto's Ferry

He left the tent of the soup kitchen, passing
A friend without speaking. A mockingbird
Freeing every song it had heard
In those last brackish hours of evening.
He lit a cigarette. Something clean
Like gin was what he was missing . . .

He walked over the gravel to the new power station
Which at night is like a chandelier
Of guttering, blank candles. He threw burlap
Over the barbed wire
And dropped into a shallow security pond.
He climbed the ladder of the smokestack, turning
His back to it, facing the wind—

Spread-eagle, he dove, falling in silence
Into the cat's cradle of live wires, discrete
Moth-sear and sage in the desert air—
The neighborhoods went black in every direction.

A 707 was coming in along the dry riverbed.
A passenger, looking down on the spreading darkness,
Saw at the center of it, a suspended
Human form on fire.
She folded her hands and buried them
In the crotch of a purple dress, vomiting

Onto the bald head of the man seated in front of her.
She said, much later, "He must have been disturbed?"
The wheels of the plane now touching the earth.
In our words,
Power was being restored to the suburbs.

First Wednesday at Heater Lawns

He had his hand up my skirt. The lights dimmed. I pushed
A pearl onion around my plate with a toothpick.
We sat behind glass, white and black tablecloths
Checkered the terraces. The storm off the desert
Made the waiters nervous; behind them
The refrigerated grandstand
Climbed to the ceiling. Outside
The greyhounds ran in the red wind.

The scotch was cold. Rain now green in the palms.
The dogs slowing
On the banked turn. Tickets being torn.
I let him put a finger inside me. Silk suit, his
Legs crossed. He leaned against me.
This is what it was to live.
Money was moving at the windows again.
I stared into the empty thrones of the old shoe-shine stands:

The red ghosts of my grandfather's friends
Sat there unforgiven, mouths open—
What had they done that I could excuse them—
Then, I realized their shame was in being dead.

An American Scene

I reach beyond the laboratory brain. The brass
Lamp with its white shade throws the shadow
Of the specimen and the gladiolus in suspension
Against the wall. The gladiolus

Is a fragment of sternum,
Not some iris which would fry in formaldehyde.
The rubber apron hangs on its nail.
There is some color here— the poster
Over the autoclave
Has five red tuna boats
Rising and falling in a black sea.

My mother is marrying again. They stand
In the photograph
Before his honeysuckle hedge in Los Angeles.
I came to Boston because of the earthquakes.
And mother's
Migraines—the light of which is religious.
Mother sincerely believes that Henry James died in 1905
In that Pullman car
Crossing the great alkali desert of Arizona. At least
He wished to is what she believes.

Here all it does is rain. The technician
From C-wing has long brown hair and hazel eyes.
Yesterday, in the middle of the night, for fun
She flattened her bare breasts
Against the window to the lab.
They looked like cow pies whitened by sun.
I stripped and turned off the lamp.
She brought two paper cups
Full of brandy . . . something the deaf Beethoven wrote

Came over her radio.
I took an old soft paperback
And tucked it under the small of her back.
It was pure lust . . .
The brain glowed in the dark above us.

At the Opening to the Underground
Cemetery at Colchis

—after Rilke

It's a great red cave of muscle
With a yellow forest for a floor.
The river rushes backwards below her.
The bridge over it is made of tortured souls.
Their bodies blue and mottled.
A hot wind up in the cottonwoods. Eurydice
Is naked. Hair cut short—
She is heavy through the shoulders.
The linen of the dead
Is still unraveling at her waist and ankles.

The god of messages has her by the hand.
Orpheus has already crossed the bridge,
His cape lit with the phosphorus rot of vegetables.
He may be frightened? He *is* serious
About leaving this place. Eurydice has failed to estimate

His impatience—that irritable glance backwards
And the wings of a god lift, even the man
Who has been eating his own liver looks up
Just as the river reverses itself, now flowing south.
Eurydice, no longer

In the shadow of Hermes,
Sees at the rough entrance to the underworld
The light of day
Pitted briefly by the figure of a man with lyre.
Crawling backwards over one another, the bridge of souls
Is receding toward shore. Hermes lifts into air and over
The water. Eurydice

Changes into the beast of sorrows—
Neck broken, her cropped head like a pendulous third breast,
She shuffles back into the yellow forest.

It helps, at this point, to picture the maenads
Making mincemeat of Orpheus.
But he's done mourning. And there will be first,
An eternity of music, visions and orgies.

THREE

Northwind Escarpment

The mirrors in the hall were a strange backwater
Of mercury and leafmold. The walnut table
Was wet with twilight. The standing radio
Had the red static of needles in a pine forest.

Outside the window, beyond the ginkgo,
Two girls with long bare legs were sinking
In the endless mudflats.
Their father in a white suit shook a stick at them.
The girls' laughter seemed a problem for him.

The tide had never withdrawn this far from the house.
Your skirt dropped to your ankles. You unbuttoned
Your blouse. In complete darkness
You walked to the kitchen and washed yourself
From the waist up. You came back
To the piano bench where we shared a cigarette.

While we slept the tide crept in
And the blistered troughs that are rowboats
Banged against one another . . .

By sunrise we had all died in the war. What's more
We always knew it was possible.

New Age at Airport Mesa

My husband was hanging wet sheets, almost in disbelief,
When he had his heart attack. It kicked him
In the neck and shoulder; the heavy linen,
Flying backwards with him, was sucked darkly
Into his mouth— he was like that Wyoming snowfield
Where the ground above the old cistern collapsed.
I was still grieving when the oleander blossomed.

So Ruth and I rented a cottage for a month. I painted
The stream and poplars. Ruth meditated
And made enough cucumber sandwiches to feed
Us and our dead husbands. She had a vision that third week
Of a naked Navajo giantess eating a peach.
It was so real that the juice of the peach
Ran down her chin and breasts striking the dust
Like a rain of nails. Ruth was delighted with her vision
Until she realized it was meaningless.

Our last afternoon in the cottage she was feeling nauseous
And I was bored
So I visited the canyon for the first time alone. I whistled
A warning to the snakes.
I found a sandstone platform above a young palo verde.
My mind wandered for I don't know how long
Until I realized I had been staring, at some distance,
At two nude women, girls really,
Kneeling before one another and touching themselves:

They began to kiss— they were both blond, it was
More like one woman and a mirror. What they did I wouldn't
Tell you. But toward the end I could even hear them.
As I listened to their cries rising above the desert,

I began to cry with them. The hot wind
Dried my tears. It dried their mouths, their whole bodies . . .

Later when I told Ruth she amazingly approved
And announced it was a vision. I agreed
So she would stop talking . . . I smiled.
Sat on the couch.
I told her I was done feeling sorry for myself.

The Clergyman's Daughter

The moose of the peninsula ate from our truck garden
Leaving us with a crazy destruction that is salad.

Once my father dreamt that we rode
On a slow carousel that played a Bach fugue,
We were not seated on painted ponies but on huge
Stuffed moose. His had a three-corner tear in its ear
Sewn with red thread and its rack was a slough of velvet.
When he told my mother his dream
She laughed, in tears, until she wet herself
Sitting on the stairs . . .

                              she cried again that night
When pine martens killed the goose.

We fished for flounder off the cliffs among the floating fields
Of pepper-dulse seaweed. We watched
That spot where the farmer
Said he saw a German U-boat surface . . .
Father says that God's perfect entreaty is the sea.
I don't believe him.

I knew
That the willow ptarmigan had nested in the long grass,
In a weathered lobster-trap that is a grotesque crate,
Carrion of broken rib cage with a double vortex of black string
Where the heart should be . . .
I would not want its old dream of a slamming

Arterial seawater inside me.

Shipwreck

Three Chinese in yellow coats stood on dunes, waist-high
In the brittle grasses. They would be foreshortened
If anyone, some Margaret ghost, was looking inland
Where the snow
Was another catastrophe of quartz, a wanton sand,
Or so the oldest of them was thinking
While all three watched masts and sail,
Just sticks and a rag, being sucked into the Atlantic.

The bodies that washed up on shore were dressed
In nightshirts. They froze and the hair of the women
Snapped off at the scalp like glass.
The three Chinese had eaten opium:
The pellucid joints of the blue crabs
Were like the icy joints of the brittle grasses.

They watched it all, though it wasn't happening . . .

Their laundry and the Quail Island foundry
Vented together fire and steam. There were dragons
Dreaming everywhere. Irish from the furnaces
Came down the dunes
And rushed past the Chinese to the bodies on the beach.
The foreman stood in the water weeping.
His friends dragged him onto land
And all seven walked toward the Chinamen
Who later, at dawn, were hanged with hotel sheets
Still warm from ironing.

So on her trip from Italy
Margaret Fuller and her child and husband were lost at sea.
Emerson sent Thoreau to comb the beach
For journals, clothing, or possibly

47

The rings. Emerson was patronizing
To her death. Hawthorne was vicious with care.
Henry James, the Master, said, "She was, at last,
Finally Italianised and shipwrecked." There were dragons
Feeding everywhere.

Safe Conduct

The snowplow was a rattling iron box
With a long chain sparking behind it.
The one curled blade raised to the air in Sanskrit.
The blue light on the floor of the cab
Was muted by a rag. The window, cracked
On my side, was sealed in the rose tint
Of a pinup from the garage.

The windshield wipers made time. The highbeams
Failed in the night,
In the revealed light that is snow.
From the back of the truck Charlie Minor,
Who stood with a shovel in a mountain of rock salt,
Coughed and yowled. My grandfather shifted gears
And we began the descent to the county roads.

The blade dropped, the lip of a snarling dog.
Coming off the hill, going fifty,
We left the hard dirt that Parker plowed
And hit the drifting snow. Eight years old,
I reached into waxpaper
For chunks of ham, some cheese and the red potatoes.
He laughed, a thermos of coffee in his hand;
Past midnight, he looked back
And I was asleep,
Propped up with a pillow of old surveyors' maps.
Charlie Minor drank from his pint of whiskey,
Yelling to my grandfather, "Sure is a bitch, Earl."
My grandfather adjusted his weight and put it to the floor.
The next morning his heart gave out.
In the barns we passed there were cows, each with a face
As distant as this world.

The Saints of Negativity

It was the first snow in memory, and
A dark morning.
The cypress trees had fallen from the skies
Like long fan feathers of the white ibis.

The patron, Piero de' Medici,
Eating his orange,
Childishly summoned Michelangelo
Back to the villa
From the Infirmary of Santo Spirito
Where the sculptor
Had dissected a fresh body, his awful
Studies in anatomy.

A huge block of snow was shaded
With skins
And the young Michelangelo
Was to make a virgin and child.
Servants to Piero, as a joke,
Had spoiled the marble
With a trickle of ox blood. Then
They paved the uncarved block
With more snow and a glaze of water.

Under the afternoon sun
Michelangelo reached the courtyard
And the snowmen of Piero's bastard children
Had sagged into large pears
Which the hungry birds sat upon . . .

Piero de' Medici, disappointed with the sun,
Had gone to bed with his first cousin

Who as a girl
Had roasted and eaten her favorite falcon.

Still in his hospital apron
Michelangelo sat in the cart
With one hand on a muddy wheel
And stared into the white stubble
Of the distant field. All he could see

Was the bearded face of the old peasant
He had undone that same morning.
He took his wrap of knives
And approached the block of snow. He threw

Off the goat skins. He told Piero later
That a woman and child were buried in snow;
That he found them, but
In the sunlight they turned to water
And wine, possibly water and blood. He didn't
Know. Make no mistake, he said,
The earth like a crust of bread absorbed them.

Easter Night, Paris

/

The paperback, its spine nearly broken,
Left open on the table, closes—first a few pages,
Then a flurry,
And, at last, the waxed jacket— it brought
To mind the slow natural death of an insect.

If, as Freud suggests
In his analysis of "little Hans," the worst famine
Begins at the other breast, at the very moment
We are first shifted to it, then
He must have intuited
That this is also the origin of feasting, the calculus
And plagues of insects—

The text says *locust*—undoubtable provision is fear,

And my wife cries in joy for the angels
Have rolled down a hillside
The capstone to an empty tomb. She was
Born in the country. I was born in Lyon.

The second coronary humbled me some.

I thought my arms were heavy with lilac blossoms,
I smelled them
Just seconds before the pain
Cramped my neck and chest. This was when I remembered
Doctor Freud dying in his London flat, at his request

They administered with a hypodermic

Two centigrams of morphine. His head lolling.
In the suburbs of Paris, in the fields, the golden locust
Begin, in season, a slow natural death:

First the wings, but just barely,
Then a flurry,
And, at last, the waxed jacket— folded, they bring
To mind the great stone reliquaries of another time
When death was not a paperback.

The Garden Asylum of Saint-Paul-de-Mausole

In the orchard the old crones sit on cane chairs.
They are like the decaying pears—some fuzz
And the strangest russet of ear wax—matter relaxed

Along a curve.

In the purple rows of charged gladiolas, the docile
Wasps are tossed about,
Almost biblical, they're making paper in their mouths.

Before the rosebank and distant cattails, bean plants
With bits of string and poles
Become the lean, sychophant monastics
To whom the asylum is willed . . .

The Abbot visits these grounds, not knowing of Van Gogh.

The Abbot, stung by wasps, died slowly of blood poisoning.
The other one, Van Gogh,
Died on our sun and was buried there in the snow.

The Desert Deportation of 1915

Our dead fathers came down to us in the river.
Thousands of fathers and grown brothers
Bobbing in the Euphrates . . .
The two generals rode their horses
Over the hill
Like happy widows on strong donkeys.

My mother loved men, I buried
Her in the river with them.
There was limitless mind in the open eyes
Of my dead mother.
I buried my little brother on the grass plain.
Dogs dug him up that night. At dawn
I buried him again—what
I could find of him—in excrement
Stolen from latrines.
The dogs would let him be. I stuck
Two dozen irises from the riverbank
In his grave, it all baked hard
In the sun that day.

One of the Turks, a cook,
Thought a little girl this smart
Should be saved.
I wish I could say they were
All cruel and disgusting.
But they gave me fruit and bread.
On the march down the valley
They left me with villagers
Who were of the Muslim faith. And
Though I was lazy, they raised me
From the dead.

Near the Bridge of Saint-Cloud

—after Rouseau

A swollen infant under a tree, rose petals
Stuck to his cheeks, heavy plaster eyelids
Clucking like false teeth in disbelief . . .

He was abandoned here by his mother
Who is a student of the East.
At sunrise she thought the reflected
Arches of the bridge over the water
Were the brass-knuckles of the Turkish Police.

She knew the shaded riverbank was a street
For the serene bourgeoisie:
And the strolling painter
And the baby, who are
One and the same, openly
Look toward us
Rather than to each other
Which would complete the painting.

The mother is now huddled in a yellow shack
In the middle of vineyards.
Her spoon in the candle flame blackens.
There's the last of the powder
On a square of paper
And a hose tourniquet the color of skin.
What she sees, unlikely muse

Inspiring mystery, is not the throne room
Of some sad Byzantine, but the metal
bitch camel of King Artabanus:
The automaton would spit and kick, was musical
Beyond comprehension,
And its right front hoof, studded with rubies,

Was used by the King to crush the skulls
Of family members who proved uninteresting.

Old Artabanus had a large ascending throne,
An elevator of gold flanked by palms.
It rose to a lapis dome
Which was eventually painted in the blood
Of another king's messenger-son
Who thought to promote a peace,
Equal to childhood, throughout the kingdoms of the East.

Coyote Creek

It was a small canyon, very small
With a low waterfall, saw-grass running
From the pool to the decaying ponderosa ridge.
The north wall, cut by water was
Pure, almost tantric. The stream ran over a red floor.
The other wall had blue lichen on it.

A rope up in the juniper. Swallows nesting
In the north wall; they *were*, I thought,
The politics of the City of God. I told them
I wouldn't trouble their babies.
I said a prayer to this place
For a friend who had lost all hope.

I am not cautious. But when my daughter
Brought me a handful of chalcedony
I helped her return it to the mud pool
Below the juniper. I told her
It would have lost its colors in the air—
We are to disturb nothing here. *I have*

Said a prayer for John.
Just then a *scare-bird* with a white stripe
Across its wings and back,
Across the fan of its tail feathers, cried
Out from the barren ridge. It reminded me
Of a sack, black
With white bones painted on it
That belonged to my grandmother. What
Kept him on the ridge

Was a force of twelve swallows with young.
I walked up the sandy path

To where my daughter sat in the car.
She was angry. My wife comforted her. *We are*

To disturb nothing here. I had
Said a prayer to water and rock.
I had refused a gift from my daughter,
And watched
The *scare-bird* sing, shifting in the dead pines
While the sun sank all at once behind him.

Amen

—for Patrick & Robert

Someone calls *Duchess*, our fawn Great Dane, back
Across the dusty road: she's nearly to the lawn
When the Buick hits her, she rolls
And then gaining her legs
Runs into the field of goldenrod where my father
Finds her; when he presses
The large folded handkerchief against the wound, it vanishes
Along with his forearm. She was months dying.

One night returning from my aunt's house, we stopped
At a light and watched a procession of cars
Coming down out of the first snow, down
Out of the mountains, returning to Connecticut. Everywhere
Roped to the hoods and bumpers were dead deer.
The man behind us honked
His horn. My father waved him on. He hit
The horn again. My father got out and spoke
With him in a voice that was frightening
Even for a man with a horn. We left the door open
And the four of us sat there in the dome light
In silence. Wanting to be fair,
I thought of squatting cavemen, sparks flying
From flints into dry yellow lichen and white smoke
Rising from Ethel Rosenberg's hair.

NORMAN DUBIE was born in Barre, Vermont, in April 1945. His poems have appeared in many magazines, including *The Paris Review*, *The New Yorker*, *The American Poetry Review*, *Antaeus*, *Field*, and *Poetry*. He has won the Bess Hokin Award of the Modern Poetry Association and fellowships from the National Endowment for the Arts, the John Simon Guggenheim Foundation, and the Ingram Merrill Foundation. He lives in Tempe, Arizona, with his wife, the poet Jeannine Savard, and their daughter, Hannah. Mr. Dubie teaches at Arizona State University.